FOCUS ON THE FAMILY PR...

Peril in the Palace

BOOK 3

MARIANNE HERING • PAUL McCUSKER
ILLUSTRATED BY DAVID HOHN

TYNDALE

FOCUS ON THE FAMILY • ADVENTURES IN ODYSSEY
TYNDALE HOUSE PUBLISHERS, INC. • CAROL STREAM, ILLINOIS

Thanks for the encouragement:

Bob Dubberley, Brock Eastman, Clark Miller, Larry Weeden, and Glenn Williams

---

Peril in the Palace
Copyright © 2011 Focus on the Family

A Focus on the Family book published by
Tyndale House Publishers, Inc., Carol Stream, Illinois 60188

Focus on the Family and Adventures in Odyssey, and their accompanying logos and designs, and The Imagination Station, are federally registered trademarks of Focus on the Family, Colorado Springs, CO 80995.

TYNDALE and Tyndale's quill logo are registered trademarks of Tyndale House Publishers, Inc.

Cover design by Michael Heath, Magnus Creative

Library of Congress Cataloging-in-Publication Data
Hering, Marianne.
  Peril in the palace / by Marianne Hering and Paul McCusker ; illustrated by David Hohn.
-- 1st ed.
    p. cm. -- (Imagination Station ; bk. #3)
  "Focus on the Family."
  Summary: Cousins Patrick and Beth travel in Mr. Whittaker's invention, the Imagination Station, to thirteenth-century China, where they meet Marco Polo and Kublai Khan and are mistaken for Christian shamans.
  [1. Space and time--Fiction. 2. Mongols--Fiction. 3. Polo, Marco, 1254-1323?--Fiction. 4. Kublai Khan, 1216-1294--Fiction. 5. Cousins--Fiction. 6. Christian life--Fiction. 7. China--History--Y?an dynasty, 1260-1368--Fiction.] I. McCusker, Paul, 1958- II. Hohn, David, 1974- ill. III. Title.
  PZ7.H431258Per 2011
  [Fic]--dc22

                                                         2010054586

ISBN 978-1-58997-629-0

Printed in the United States of America
3 4 5 6 7 8 9/16 15 14 13 12 11

For manufacturing information regarding this product, please call 1-800-323-9400.

Other books in this series

Contents

Prologue

There is an old house in the town of Odyssey. It's called Whit's End. Kids love it. It has an ice-cream shop. It also has a lot of rooms with games and displays.

There are exciting things to do at Whit's End. Kids have fun and learn there.

Mr. Whittaker owns Whit's End. He is a kind yet mysterious inventor. One of his inventions is the Imagination Station.

The Imagination Station lets kids see history

in person. It's a lot like a time machine.

One day the Imagination Station broke. Mr. Whittaker didn't know why. He tried to fix the machine in his workshop.

Two cousins, Patrick and Beth, came to visit him. Patrick and Beth are eight years old.

Patrick touched the Imagination Station. Suddenly the machine lit up!

Mr. Whittaker was surprised. He told

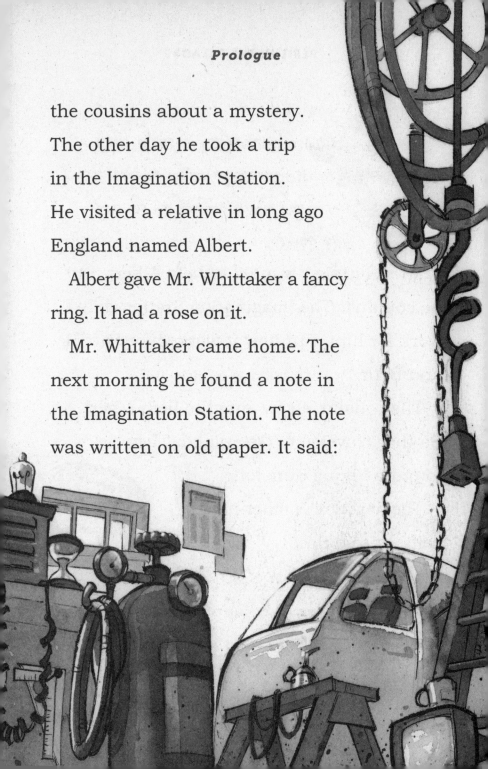

the cousins about a mystery.
The other day he took a trip
in the Imagination Station.
He visited a relative in long ago
England named Albert.

Albert gave Mr. Whittaker a fancy
ring. It had a rose on it.

Mr. Whittaker came home. The
next morning he found a note in
the Imagination Station. The note
was written on old paper. It said:

To save Albert, I need a Viking Sunstone before the new moon. Or Lord Darkthorn will lock him inside the tower.

Mr. Whittaker wanted to help Albert. But he couldn't. The Imagination Station didn't work for him. But now it worked for Patrick and Beth.

The cousins also wanted to help Albert. So they traveled to Greenland. They found a Viking Sunstone.

The next day another note came. It said this:

More trouble for Albert. Lord Darkthorn is angry. The Roman monk's silver cup is missing. We need it before the new moon. May God be with you.

Again Patrick and Beth asked to help.

They visited ancient Rome. They were chased by a tiger. And the cousins found the silver cup.

A strange thing happened in Rome. An English knight arrived in the Imagination Station. The cousins were amazed. How could a knight use the Imagination Station?

The knight gave them a message:

"You must tell Mr. Whittaker to search for the golden tablet of Kublai Khan."

Now Beth and Patrick are off on another adventure. They need to meet Kublai Khan and find his golden tablet.

They also want answers to some puzzling questions:

Who is writing the notes?

What is a golden tablet?

Who is Kublai Khan?

They are about to find out.

The Mongols

On Wednesday, Patrick and Beth were ready to go to China. They were all set to find the golden tablet.

Patrick had on a bright blue tunic with an orange border. The toes of his shoes curled up at the ends.

Beth wore an orange dress. It was made of fine silk. Her shoes were just like Patrick's.

"Those costumes are great," Mr. Whittaker said. "You look just like Mongol children."

"Did you say *mongrel*?" Beth asked. "That's what my dog is."

Mr. Whittaker smiled. His kind eyes twinkled behind his round glasses.

"No, Beth," Mr. Whittaker said. "I said *Mon-gol*. The Mongols ruled all of China in the thirteenth century. Today their country is called *Mongolia*."

"I've heard that word," said Patrick. "There's a Mongolian barbecue on Main Street. That restaurant cooks the best meat in town."

"Well," Mr. Whittaker said, "in Kublai Khan's time, Mongols were the best *fighters* in town."

"Uh-oh," said Beth.

"Don't be afraid," Patrick said. "I'll protect you."

Beth frowned.

"How can you protect me?" she asked. "You don't know anything about Kublai Khan. What if he's nasty and mean?"

Patrick looked at Mr. Whittaker. "Is he?" Patrick asked.

"Well, *khan* means emperor," Mr. Whittaker said. "So he was one of the most powerful—and richest—men in the world at the time."

"Emperors can be nasty and mean," Beth said.

"They can be," Mr. Whittaker said. "But Kublai was also known for his love of art, astronomy, and knowledge. That will work in your favor."

"How?" Beth asked.

Mr. Whittaker said, "I prepared some

things for you to take with you."

He walked over to a large closet and rummaged around inside. He came back with three things: a colorful wool bag, a box of very long nails, and a hammer.

"Nails?" Beth said. "Why?"

Mr. Whittaker held up a nail. "Kublai Khan likes new things. He's never seen one of these."

"He hasn't seen a nail?" Beth asked.

Mr. Whittaker put the nail in Beth's hand.

"No," Mr. Whittaker said. "So this should please him."

"If you say so," she said. Beth frowned and then studied the nail. It had a square head and a long shaft. It was almost a spike.

She touched the tip of the nail. "It's

sharp," she said.

"Keep the nails in the wool bag until you need them," Mr. Whittaker said. He put the hammer in the bag too, and he handed it to Patrick.

"Whoa!" Patrick said. "This is really heavy." He looked at Mr. Whittaker. "What else is in here?"

"You'll see," Mr. Whittaker said. "There are several gifts inside. Each one is wrapped separately. And each one has a tag on it. Read the tags to figure out when to use them. Give away the first gift when you meet someone with a famous name."

"We're going to meet someone famous?" Beth asked.

"He wasn't famous then," Mr. Whittaker said. "But you'll recognize his name when you hear it."

Beth and Patrick looked at each other. Their eyes lit up with curiosity.

"Shall we start the adventure?" Mr. Whittaker asked. He waved a hand toward the Imagination Station.

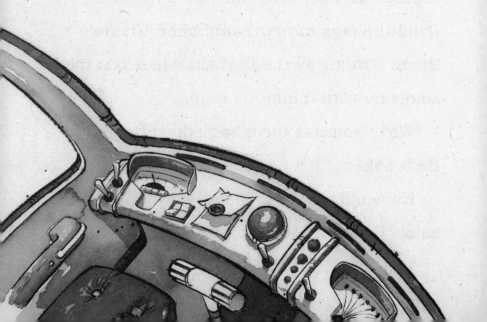

The Imagination Station

Beth and Patrick climbed into the Imagination Station. They sat in its comfortable black seats.

Beth looked at the dashboard. The two notes about Albert were still there, but the silver cup was gone.

"Did you send the cup back to England?" Beth asked. "It's not here."

Mr. Whittaker shook his head. "I'm sure someone from Albert's time took it," he said.

"Was it the knight?" Patrick asked.

"Probably," Mr. Whittaker said. "Somehow he's able to use the machine."

"You mean without your knowing," Patrick said.

"I control the machine with my computer when *you* travel," Mr. Whittaker said. "I'm still not sure how he's making it work."

The cousins shrugged. They didn't know either.

Beth thought that Mr. Whittaker looked a little sad.

"What's wrong?" she asked him.

"I wish you didn't have to make all these trips," Mr. Whittaker said. "I should be the one to help Albert."

"We don't mind," Patrick said. "How many kids get to meet Vikings—or a Roman emperor?"

"When can you travel in the Imagination Station again?" Beth asked Mr. Whittaker.

"I don't know," Mr. Whittaker said. "For some reason, the Imagination Station's computer is keeping me out. It may have something to do with the remote control I left in England."

Mr. Whittaker reached inside the Imagination Station. When he did, the fancy ring from Albert appeared on his finger.

Patrick pointed to the ring. "It's funny how it only shows up in here," he said. "What good is wearing it?"

Mr. Whittaker smiled and said, "Albert wanted to swap rings. And I couldn't say no."

"Swap rings?" Beth said.

"Yes," said Mr. Whittaker. "I gave him a family ring, and Albert gave me this one."

Mr. Whittaker tapped the dashboard and said, "Press the red button when you're ready."

"We'll say hello to the knight if we see him again," Patrick said.

Mr. Whittaker smiled and closed the Imagination Station's door.

Patrick reached out and pushed the red button.

The Imagination Station started to shake. Then it rumbled.

Beth clenched her teeth and closed her eyes.

Patrick imagined that he was in a jet plane. He pushed his body into the seat and waited. The machine jerked forward.

The rumble grew louder.

The machine whirled.

The Horses

Patrick and Beth opened their eyes.

Patrick and Beth were surrounded by horses. Tan, brown, black, and gray horses. Their heads were large, but their legs were short. They nuzzled the ground, eating grass. Their breath blew out in small gusts.

They hardly noticed Patrick and Beth. Only one horse lifted its head when the Imagination Station faded from sight.

Patrick held the wool bag. Its long strap

was draped over his shoulder.

The cousins looked around in silence.

They were in the shade of a tall cliff. The cliff was rugged and red. It went straight up like a building twenty stories tall.

The rest of the area was pale and sandy. Scrubby bushes and patches of short grass pushed up through the sand. Hilly plains with longer grass were in the distance.

The cousins did not see any people or buildings.

"Which way should we go?" Beth asked.

Patrick shrugged.

A small black horse moved toward Beth.

"It's so cute," she said.

It nudged her with its nose. She patted it on the head.

"Maybe it wants to give us a ride," Patrick

said.

"That would be stealing," Beth said.

Suddenly all the horses lifted their heads. Their ears pricked up.

The black horse snorted.

"What's wrong, horsie?" Beth asked.

The horses looked in one direction.

The cousins followed their gaze.

Seven men on horseback rounded the cliff's base. The horses galloped through the sand.

"Do you think the men are friendly?" Beth asked. She wanted to hide until she could be sure.

"Maybe they can help us find Kublai Khan," said Patrick.

"I don't know—" Beth started to say.

But Patrick waved his arms as if he were doing jumping jacks. "Over here," he shouted. "Come this way!"

The horsemen slowed. They gathered together in a group. Beth thought they must be talking to one another.

All at once, the horses galloped toward the cousins. The horses' hooves drummed against the earth.

"It worked," said Patrick.

"I hope they're friendly," Beth said, worried.

As the riders came closer, Beth could see them better. They were dressed in tan tunics. Their long braids of hair flopped in the wind.

The horses' saddle blankets were rainbow colored. The horses' manes were cut short.

The horsemen moved closer. They still rode at a full gallop.

"They're not slowing down," Beth said.

Patrick put up a hand to wave. "Hi!" he called to them.

Beth stepped toward Patrick. The riders didn't look like they were going to stop. And they were close. *Too* close.

"Watch out, Patrick!" Beth called.

It was too late. A horse came alongside them. The rider leaned sideways and grabbed Beth under the arms. He pulled her up onto the saddle.

"Put me down!" Beth shouted.

Beth gasped and tried to twist away. She wanted to jump off. But the horseman held her in place with a strong arm.

"Stop!" Patrick said. He was busy watching Beth, and he didn't see the other rider. The man rode close to him. He wrapped an arm around his waist and drew him up.

"Put me down!" he shouted at the horseman.

The man paid no attention. He dropped Patrick onto the front of the saddle. He kicked at the horse to speed up.

The man looked grim. He carried arrows and a bow on his back.

This can't be happening, Patrick thought. *We're being kidnapped by Mongol warriors!*

The Cooking Fire

Patrick and Beth rode with the Mongol warriors for a long time. The horses ran fast on the flat and grassy plains.

In the distance, the cousins could see the Great Wall of China. It twisted through the mountains like a giant snake.

After an hour of riding, Beth and Patrick were closer to the wall. Beth noted that it was made out of large yellow stone blocks. It had a square tower. A wide moat blocked the front of the wall.

Beth hoped the warriors would stop at the moat. They didn't.

Instead, the horses clomped over a wood bridge. It took them over the water. They came to a metal gate in the wall.

The metal gate was raised by Mongol men on top of the wall. Next, two wood doors opened. The Mongol warriors, with Patrick and Beth, passed through a tunnel.

The cousins' legs were tired from riding. Yet it was another hour before the Mongols stopped at their camp.

The camp was set up in the middle of tall grass. Several saddled horses, sheep, and oxen grazed nearby.

A round, tentlike house sat at the center of the camp. Beth thought the house looked like a giant cake. The outside was the color of caramel frosting. She had seen pictures of Mongol houses in books at school.

A small fire burned a few feet from the house. A large cooking pot hung over the flames.

The Mongol warriors let Beth and Patrick slide off their horses.

Beth's legs felt like jelly. "Ow," she said. "My legs are sore."

Patrick landed with a *thud*.

"My legs are numb," Patrick said. "I think they fell asleep."

He rubbed his legs. "Ooh! Pins and needles!" he said. He bent his knees and jumped up and down.

His movement startled a nearby horse. It neighed. Patrick waved his hands at it.

"Go away," he said.

One of the Mongols shouted at Patrick.

The horse reared up with a whinny.

"You're scaring the horse," Beth said.

Suddenly the horse rushed toward
Patrick. Its mouth was wide open, and its
lips were curled back. Yellow teeth showed.

"Yikes!" Patrick said.

He quickly stepped back. He tripped over
a rock. The wool bag on his shoulder fell
sideways. The weight pulled him off balance.

"Watch out!" Beth called.

Patrick stumbled toward the fire! He was
only one step away from the flames.

Patrick yanked up his leg to avoid the fire.
He took a giant scissor step right over the pit.

Patrick's other foot kicked the large pot. The
pot rocked back and forth. The liquid inside
splashed over the rim and put out the flames.

The Mongol warriors shouted, "Aiii."

"He jumped over the fire!" said the Mongol warrior who had picked up Beth.

Another one said, "He is full of evil!"

The whole camp of Mongol men rushed toward Patrick. They formed a circle around him.

Beth hurried to reach Patrick. She tried to squeeze between two warriors. But they blocked her.

Beth heard Patrick say to the men, "I had to jump over the fire. What's the big deal?"

The men tightened their circle. Their hands were raised in fists. Beth was afraid.

Then a deep voice from behind Beth spoke. It said in a loud voice, "Mighty warriors! Let us talk!"

Beth turned around to see who had spoken.

It was a tall young man. His brown hair hung to his shoulders. He had a short beard. He wore the Mongol warrior tunic, but he also wore a floppy, blue velvet hat.

The men slowly stepped away from Patrick. They turned to face the tall man.

Beth rushed to Patrick. He was curled up like a ball. His arms were crossed over his head to protect it.

"I don't like this place very much," he said as Beth helped him up. Patrick was covered with sand, but otherwise he was unharmed.

The man in the velvet hat waved for them to come behind him.

"Jumping over a cooking fire is against the Mongol law," he said gently to them.

"But . . . but I was falling," Patrick said. "I almost got burned. It was an accident."

"The boy is clearly a stranger and has made a mistake," the man said to the warriors.

The Mongol who had grabbed Beth stepped out of the crowd. He came forward and bowed to the new man. He bowed so low that his forehead touched the ground.

Then he stood up and said, "The boy and the girl are evil."

"Why do you call them evil, Koke?" the man asked.

Koke said, "They suddenly appeared in the desert. They left no tracks. They had no animals to ride."

The man in the blue hat looked at Patrick and Beth. "You appeared without making tracks? Did you fall from the sky?"

Suddenly Koke pointed at Beth. He said,

"And this girl tried to steal a horse."

Beth gasped.

"I only patted him on the head!" she said. "Is that against the law too?"

Koke sneered at her.

The Mongol scowled. "There is the matter of the fire."

The man drew Beth and Patrick close. He said, "These children aren't Mongols. You can't expect them to know or understand your laws."

The young man ruffled Patrick's blond hair. He gave the cousins a comforting smile.

"We demand that they be punished," Koke said. "In the name of Kublai Khan, we must have justice."

The young man gave a half bow. His blue

hat flopped when he leaned over.

"Ah," he said, "you call on the name of Kublai Khan. And . . . so do I."

The young man reached inside a leather bag hanging from his belt. He pulled out a flat object. It was about a foot long and three inches wide. The edges were rounded. It had strange writing on it. It gleamed in the sun. It looked like pure gold.

Beth gasped and looked at Patrick.

"Wow," Patrick said. "That's the golden tablet!"

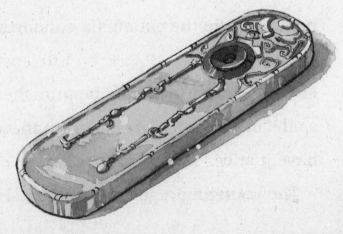

Marco Polo

The group of Mongol warriors saw the golden tablet.

"Ooh," they said.

Then the tall man said, "Kublai Khan gave my family this tablet. With it, he has given me his authority. I order you to leave the children unharmed."

The tall man leaned his head toward the children. His blue hat now flopped sideways.

"Go into the *ger*," he whispered.

"The what?" Patrick asked.

He motioned toward the tent-house. "There," he said. "I'll be right behind you."

The cousins obeyed quickly. They didn't want to stay outside with the angry warriors.

When they entered the tent, Patrick and Beth couldn't see very well. There was only a dim light from a small fire in the center of the tent.

The ger's walls were made from wool felt. They were decorated with colorful wool rugs. Wood beams held up the roof.

Just as the tall man had said, he followed them inside.

Beth and Patrick saw him tuck the golden tablet into his tunic. Then he put his hands on his hips. He looked straight at the cousins.

"What are you doing in the middle of the Mongolian desert?" he asked.

The cousins looked at each other. Neither knew how to answer.

The man eyed them. "Where did you come from? How did you get here?"

Beth heard Patrick swallow hard. She knew what he was thinking. Would this man believe them if they told him the truth?

Beth decided to try. "We are here because of an English knight," she said. "He sent us to meet Kublai Khan."

"A knight from England?" the man asked. He frowned. "Is he planning a crusade against the Mongols?"

"What's a crusade?" Patrick asked.

The young man gave Patrick a curious look.

"You haven't heard of the Crusades?" the

man asked. He touched two fingers to his forehead lightly.

Beth sighed.

"A crusade is a religious war," she said to Patrick. "Knights did—do—a lot of fighting in the Holy Land. Our friend, the knight, sent us on an errand—not a crusade."

The man said, "And what is your errand?"

"We need to find a golden tablet," said Patrick. "Like the one you have."

"Aah, that is a difficult errand. Only someone in the khan's family may give you a golden tablet." He took the tablet out and tapped it. "This one was given to my father and uncle when they came here eight years ago."

Beth studied the man more carefully. "Where are you from?" she asked.

The man took off his blue hat. He gave Beth a slight bow. "I come from Italy," he said.

"Italy is far away," Patrick said.

The man nodded and said, "I traveled three years to get here."

"Three years!" Patrick said. "Why did it take so long?"

The man looked at him with a small smile. "I don't know how to make boats, camels, or horses go any faster," he said.

"It's not like they have airplanes," Beth said softly to Patrick.

Patrick flushed with embarrassment.

"Kublai Khan's men met me in the desert," he said. "They will bring me to the Great Khan. I have gifts for him."

"We have a gift for Kublai Khan too," Beth said.

"Then come with me," the man said. He smiled. "It would be wise for us to stick together."

"My name is Beth," she said. "This is my cousin Patrick."

The man gave Beth and Patrick a little bow. He clicked his boot heels and said, "I am Marco Polo."

The First Gift

"Marco Polo!" Patrick cried out.

He was excited. Here was the foreigner Mr. Whittaker said they would meet.

Patrick said, "I've heard your name at the pool—"

Beth gently bumped Patrick's ribs with her elbow.

"He means at *school*," she said quickly. "You're a famous traveler."

Marco looked confused. He scratched

his forehead.

"Perhaps you mean my father, Niccolò," Marco said. "Or my uncle Amaffeo. They have traveled far more than I."

Just then two men stepped inside the ger.

"Ah," Marco said, "here they are now. Children, meet my father and my uncle."

The cousins politely greeted the men. They were older. They wore the same kind of hats as Marco.

"So, you're the mysterious desert visitors," Amaffeo said. "The Mongol warriors warned us about you."

"We heard you were evil," Niccolò said.

He smiled in a friendly way. Beth could tell he wasn't worried about them at all.

"We want to meet Kublai Khan," Patrick said to him. "We didn't mean to cause trouble."

Amaffeo said, "Good! We're almost ready to leave. We must pack the gifts for Kublai Khan."

"Gifts!" Patrick said. "I almost forgot."

Patrick remembered to check the wool bag. He could give the first gift to Marco.

Patrick looked inside the bag. It held several gifts. The one on top was a rectangle. It was wrapped in red paper. The tag on it said, "To Marco Polo."

Patrick handed the package to Marco.

"This is for you," Patrick said. "A gift from the kingdom of Odyssey."

Beth and Patrick smiled at each other.

Marco carefully took off the wrapping paper.

"It's a book," Marco said. He held up the book for all to see. Then he flipped through the pages.

"The pages are blank!" Marco said.

"It's a diary," Beth said.

"Do we have a quill and ink?" asked Marco.

Amaffeo said, "We do. And such a quill!"
He walked to one wall of the ger. He sorted
through some boxes that were neatly
stacked.

"Ta-da!" Amaffeo said. "I made this quill
myself. I found the feather in the desert."

Amaffeo held up a black-and-white
feather. It was about four feet long. The
feather's shaft was as thick as a pinkie
finger. The tip was black from ink.

"Wow," Beth said. "A pen made from a

feather. The bird that lost it must have been huge!"

"A giant!" said Niccolò. "I have seen the great eagles. They nest high in the cliffs. The Mongol men call them *rocs*. They are big enough to carry a sheep over a mountain."

Beth gasped.

"Oh, that is nothing," Amaffeo said. "I have seen a roc pick up an elephant!"

Patrick laughed. "An elephant?" he said. "That's impossible!"

"Believe it, boy," Marco said. He looked Patrick straight in the eyes. "This is a strange and wonderful land. Mongol warriors say they have seen a roc destroy a warship."

Beth was sure the men were joking.

But still, she thought, *this long feather came from something large.*

Beth wondered how the quill worked.

"Marco," she said, "why don't you write your name in the book?"

"A good idea," Marco said. "I'll write a title as well. Uncle Amaffeo? The inkwell, please."

Uncle Amaffeo rummaged around their crates. He brought out a small box. Inside was a bottle with black ink. He took off the bottle's cap.

Marco took out a knife and sharpened the tip of the giant quill to a point. He dipped the point in the bottle of ink. With the long feather resting on his shoulder, he wrote his name on the page. Then he wrote these words: *The Travels of Marco Polo.*

Beth watched with awe. Marco's writing was curly and beautiful.

Marco blew on the ink to help it dry. Then

he closed the book.

"Now," Marco said. "We must get on with our travels."

Beth, Patrick, and the three Italians stepped outside the ger.

Mongol men were taking down the camp. The fire pit had been covered with sand. The cooking pot was gone. Six oxen had been hooked up to a large wood cart. A handful of men approached the ger. They began to take it apart.

"What are they doing with the house?" Patrick asked.

Amaffeo said, "The Mongol men will place it on the oxen to carry it to the palace."

"It's like a heavy tent," Patrick said.

"Won't we get to stay in the khan's palace?" Beth asked. She was looking forward to seeing it.

"That's up to the khan," Marco said. "He may not like us."

"Maybe he'll like our gifts," Beth said.

"I hope so," Marco said.

A Mongol warrior brought four horses forward.

The three Italian men attached bags to the horses' saddles. Then each got on his horse.

Patrick boosted Beth onto their horse. Then Beth pulled Patrick up into the saddle. Their horse's bridle was tied to the saddle of Marco's horse. All the cousins had to do was hang on.

"We go east," Amaffeo said. He pointed off in the distance. "The palace is that way."

All at once the horses started to gallop.

"Yee-haw!" Patrick shouted. "Kublai Khan, here we come!"

The Palace

The Italian travelers and the cousins rode to Shangdu city. Patrick winced at every bump and thump. His whole body hurt from the horse ride.

The summer sun was setting in the palace courtyard. In minutes darkness would come.

"Look at the moon," Patrick said to Beth, pointing. They both thought about Albert and wondered if he were safe.

The palace looked like the Chinese houses

they had seen in movies. Everything was red or gold. The roofs sloped downward and then lifted at the corners.

Patrick could not see any gardens. But he could smell them. Sweet flower perfume and the scent of rich dirt filled the air.

The cousins got off their horse.

A young Chinese servant suddenly appeared in the courtyard. Patrick was startled because he hadn't heard any footsteps.

The servant wore a knee-length silk tunic with pants. He bowed. He then untied the horse's bridle and led the horse away.

"How did they know we were here?" Patrick asked.

"The khan knows everything that happens in his land," Marco said. "He has spies."

The three Italians were busy unpacking

their horses. More Chinese servants came
and helped them.

A Mongol servant spoke to the Polos.

"Kublai Khan waits," the servant said. "He
longs for news from Niccolò and Amaffeo Polo."

The servant's skin was very light. He wore
his hair like the Mongol warriors. But he
had a tall hat that looked like a box. His
shoes were cloth, not leather. And his tunic
was made of thin silk.

"But we stink of horses," Niccolò said. "We
can't meet the khan now. We need a bath
first."

The palace servant shook his head.

"Love has cut off its nose," the servant
said simply.

"Huh?" Patrick asked.

Marco laughed and said, "He means that

Kublai Khan won't care about the smell."

"Kublai Khan's heart is heavy," the servant said. "He has waited eight years. He feared you were dead."

Amaffeo made up his mind. "Let's go to Kublai Khan's court," he said. "I also long to greet my old friend."

The servant led them inside the palace.

Patrick and Beth were amazed. Beth's mouth hung open.

"Do you see?" she said to Patrick.

"I see!" Patrick said.

The floors were covered with gold bricks. The walls were made of wood beams and more gold bricks.

Beth tugged on Niccolò's sleeve.

She pointed at the bricks.

"Is . . . is that real gold?" she asked.

"Why, of course," Niccolò said. "The khan wants—and gets—the very best."

Patrick looked at the high ceiling. He was surprised at all the empty space. From the outside, the palace looked tall enough for three stories. However, the entire building was only one level.

The cousins and the men came to a huge carved door. It was tall and wide enough for two elephants. The doors to the throne room swung open.

Niccolò, Amaffeo, and Marco all slowed down. They stood side by side. Beth and Patrick came alongside them.

Beth's eyes were wide with wonder. The room was richly decorated. Colorful rugs, vases, paintings, and tapestries filled the room. The furniture was carved with detailed patterns. Some of it was painted gold.

In the center of the room was a large white throne. An old man sat on the throne. He wore white clothes. White animal skins draped from his chair. Around the khan stood men, women, and even a few children. All of them wore fine silk clothes and tall hats.

One of the children was a young girl. She looked at Beth with a curious smile. Beth smiled back.

A servant blew a small trumpet four times.

Another servant shouted, "Behold, the Great Khan!"

The Polos stepped forward. Patrick and Beth followed. They slowly approached the throne.

Kublai Kahn

"What are we supposed to do?" Beth whispered.

They had never met a Mongol khan before.

"Do whatever Marco does," Patrick said.

So they did what the Italians did.

When the three men dropped to their knees, so did Patrick and Beth.

When the three men bowed their foreheads to the floor, so did Patrick and Beth.

They did that four times to show respect.

And then the old man in white spoke.

"Stand!" Kublai Khan said.

Beth and Patrick scrambled to their feet. The three Italians rose more slowly.

"My eyes see only five people," Kublai Khan said. His voice was rough, as if he had swallowed sand.

"Amaffeo, Niccolò," Kublai Khan said, "eight years ago I asked for one hundred Christian teachers. You brought only one young man and two small children. Where are the teachers?"

Niccolò coughed to clear his throat. Drops of sweat popped out on his forehead. Beth thought Niccolò looked worried.

"Your Excellency," Niccolò said, "we bring you some holy oil from Jerusalem."

Niccolò held out a pretty gold jar. A servant came to carry the oil to Kublai Khan.

The khan studied the jar. He opened it and sniffed the oil inside. Then he poured a few drops on his fingers.

Kublai Khan frowned.

"Does this oil have any special power?" Kublai Khan asked. "Will it make me young again? Will it turn sand into gold?"

Niccolò shook his head. "No, Your Excellency," he said.

"Is this all you bring to me?" Kublai Khan asked. "Worthless oil?"

Amaffeo answered this time. "We also bring a letter from Gregory the Tenth, the leader of our church," he said. He pulled a parchment out of his tunic.

Amaffeo read the letter out loud. It said nice things about Kublai Khan. It told about the Crusades going on in Jerusalem. Gregory the Tenth was sorry he could not send Christian teachers to China. He said he needed his teachers in Europe.

Kublai Khan frowned.

Amaffeo offered the paper to him, but the khan waved his hand. He did not want it.

"Why doesn't your God help the Christians?" Kublai Khan asked. "Why doesn't the Christian God smash your enemies?"

Niccolò and Amaffeo were silent.

Patrick and Beth looked at each other. "Someone should say something," Patrick whispered to her.

"What did you say?" the khan called out

to Patrick. He waved. "Come closer. Speak so I may hear you."

Patrick took two steps toward the white throne. His knees were shaking.

"Will this child answer my question since the adults cannot?" Kublai Khan said. "Speak, boy! Why doesn't your Christian God destroy your enemies?"

"He has destroyed our greatest enemy," Patrick said in a shaky voice.

"Oh? Which enemy is that?" the khan asked.

"Jesus Christ destroyed death. He rose from the grave! Those who believe in Him will live forever."

"Bah!" Kublai Khan said. "My uncle was a Christian. My mother was a Christian. Both are now dead."

"But they're alive in heaven," Patrick said. "And you can live there too, if *you* ask for forgiveness—"

Patrick was cut off by Kublai Khan's laughter. He let out a deep roll of gusty hah-hahs.

Then the khan stopped laughing and stroked his beard. He said, "I want to *see* what your God can do for me. I want to live in *this world* forever. And I want an army that will never suffer defeat. I want glory."

Patrick opened his mouth to argue, but Niccolò put a hand on Patrick's shoulder. He leaned his head close to Patrick's ear.

"He only understands what he can see," Niccolò whispered. "He believes he will go to the afterlife as a warrior. The Mongols will bury him with arrows and horses."

Kublai Khan snapped his fingers. He motioned toward a group of men at the side of the room. They wore long yellow robes and yellow turbans. The men came forward and circled Kublai Khan's throne.

"We will see who has power," Kublai Khan said. "Your God or the Mongol shamans."

The Yellow Lamas

"Who are those men?" Beth whispered.

"Those are the yellow lamas," Niccolò whispered to the cousins. "They are the Mongol religious men. The people also call them *shamans*."

The shamans talked quietly to Kublai Khan. After they were done, the men bowed to him.

Then Kublai Khan spoke to the Polos and the cousins.

"The yellow lamas are powerful," Kublai

Khan said. "They have more power than Christians. Watch and see."

One of the yellow lamas walked to a nearby table. He pushed it toward the throne.

The shaman set a metal cup in the center of the table. He placed a large metal pitcher next to the cup.

Another shaman came to the table. He stood on the other side.

Another yellow lama took out a small flute. He began to play a strange song.

Beth didn't like the music. It sounded off-key and creepy.

The shamans waved their arms to the music. Their eyes glowed with emotion. The men—as if in a trance—stared at the metal pitcher.

The Polos and the cousins stepped forward to get a better look.

The metal pitcher lifted off the table. The pitcher floated in the air. Beth gasped.

The flute player's notes rose higher. He played the music faster and faster.

The shamans moved their arms above the pitcher. Their hands made circle shapes. The metal pitcher now tilted. It poured a red liquid into the cup.

Marco Polo's face turned white as salt. His hands shook.

"Impossible," Marco whispered. "What is this magic?"

Patrick watched with an open mouth.

Beth watched the yellow lamas carefully. Then she leaned toward Patrick. "That's not magic," she whispered.

"Then what is it?" Patrick asked.

She smiled and said, "It's *magnets*."

The Floating Pitcher

Everyone in the room watched the floating pitcher.

Beth had an idea. She opened Patrick's wool bag and took out some of the strong nails Mr. Whittaker had given them.

"What are you doing?" Patrick asked.

"I'm going to prove the shamans are using magnets," said Beth.

Beth realized the Italians and the khan were looking at her. The flute player stopped playing.

"Child! You are showing disrespect!" Amaffeo said. He was alarmed.

"Kublai Khan challenged us," Beth said. "I want to show how those shamans are doing their trick."

The khan leaned forward in his throne. "Trick?" he asked. "You say my shamans are doing tricks?"

Beth faced Kublai Khan. "I think they're using magnets," she said.

The shamans were distracted. They stepped away from the table and turned to Beth. The metal pitcher and cup crashed down. The pitcher hit the floor and bounced sideways. Liquid spilled all over the gold bricks. The shamans glared at her.

"What are magnets?" Kublai Khan asked.

"Magnets are special rocks that pull on metal," she said.

The khan looked at the shamans. "Do you know what she is saying?"

The shamans bowed slightly. "No, Great Khan," one said.

"Be careful, Beth," Patrick said softly.

"The magnets may be hidden in the shamans' big sleeves," she whispered.

"Do not test the shamans!" Kublai Khan said. "They will get angry. They will cast an evil spell on you."

"If their spells are like their tricks, then I'm not afraid," Beth said. She wasn't afraid of them. But she was afraid of being wrong.

"Well?" the khan called out. "I will reward the person who uncovers a trick."

Beth bowed to the khan. "Ask the

shamans to hold out their arms," she said. "Then I can test their powers."

The khan waved a hand at the shamans to obey. They looked worried.

"But, Great Khan—" one of the shamans said.

"Hold out your arms!" the khan said.

The shamans stretched out their arms.

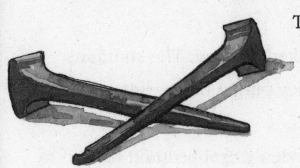 The large sleeves of their robes faced Beth.

"Take some of the nails," Beth said quickly to Patrick. She gave him a handful.

"What do you want me to do?" Patrick asked.

Beth said, "We'll toss the nails at their sleeves—on the count of three."

Patrick nodded.

"One . . . two . . . three," Beth said.

They tossed the long nails toward the shamans' sleeves.

The nails scattered in the air. Then they seemed to dangle in midair, as if hung from strings.

Everyone looked amazed. The shamans were afraid. They pulled their arms back behind them.

The nails suddenly dropped and tinkled to the floor.

Beth looked at Kublai Khan. She said, "You see?"

Kublai Khan did not look happy.

The Chicken

Kublai Khan stood up. He was a round man.
His stomach looked like a beach ball. His
white tunic hung like a tent around him.

He motioned for the lead lama to step
forward.

The lama obeyed.

"Lift up your sleeves," Kublai Khan said.

The lama didn't move.

The khan scowled at him.

The lama slowly lifted his sleeves. Small

leather bands were attached to his arms. Each band was covered in magnets.

"Bring those long, pointed sticks," the khan said to Patrick and Beth.

The cousins gathered up the strong nails and brought them forward.

Kublai Khan took one and held it near the shaman's magnetic arms.

"I feel something," the khan said.

He let go of the nail. It slammed against one of the magnets.

"These are mere *rocks*?" the khan asked.

"Yes. They have a positive and a negative force," Beth said. "A person can do fun tricks with magnets and metal."

The khan took another nail and peered at it. Then he looked at the bands on the shaman's arms.

"We have seen your power," the khan said to the shaman. His voice was cold. "You may go."

The yellow lamas bowed and hurried back to their place. They took the cup and pitcher with them.

"Are you a Christian shaman?" Kublai Khan asked Beth.

"I am *not* a shaman," Beth said. "It's science. That's all."

He held up the nail. "And what are these long sticks?"

"They are just nails, sir," Beth said. "We brought them as gifts."

The khan's eyes narrowed. He studied a nail carefully. "Do the metal sticks have special powers?" Kublai Khan asked.

"No," Beth said, "but they're very useful. They hold things together—especially wood."

"That is why we have notches," the khan said. He pointed to the ceiling beams above them.

"Our Chinese craftsmen use notches and brackets," he said. "The Mongols use rope."

Kublai Khan held up the nail again. "What good is this?" he asked.

Patrick came forward and gave a slight bow. He held the hammer in his hand.

"Great Khan," Patrick said, "this long stick makes things stay together. You can build things faster with them."

Beth was grateful for his help.

Patrick said, "You see, the pointed part goes through wood. It holds two pieces of wood together."

Patrick took the hammer and a nail to the table. He pounded the nail into the little table. It went straight through the top and into a leg.

Kublai Khan motioned toward a group of men, who stood against the wall.

The three men had small silk caps on their heads. They had thin, pointy moustaches and beards. Their eyes were dark in color but bright with interest.

The three men inspected the table in silence. One by one each shook his head.

"Bad in earthquake," one of the smart men said.

"Bad luck," said the next.

The last man scowled as if sucking on a lemon.

"Blah!" he said. "Not the Chinese way."

The Italians looked at the cousins with worried expressions.

"This isn't working," Beth said softly to Patrick. "What other gifts do we have?"

Patrick shrugged and then dug inside the wool bag again. He found a small package. He showed it to Beth.

The tag read, "Show this to Kublai Khan."

Patrick tore off the wrapping paper.

Inside was a small white chicken. It had a red comb on its head. It had stiff yellow feet. A little key stuck out of its back.

A windup toy?

Patrick and Beth looked at each other.

What was Mr. Whittaker thinking? Beth wondered.

But it was the only thing they had.

"Here is something you might like," Patrick said. "Watch this!"

All eyes turned to Patrick. He twisted the

knob a few times. Then he set the chicken on the table.

It made a soft whirring sound. The little feet hopped forward. The little beak moved toward the ground. It hopped and pecked, hopped and pecked. Then it stopped and crowed.

Cock-a-doodle-doo!

All of the people around the khan stepped back. The shamans suddenly cried out and ran off.

The Chinese servants and the khan's wise men huddled together. They were frightened.

Even the Mongols

looked wide-eyed.

The Mongol warriors lifted their weapons. Would they attack the chicken?

Kublai Khan sat down on his throne. His eyes stayed fixed on the chicken.

"You are shamans indeed," Kublai Khan said. "You have power over an evil bird spirit."

The Mongol Messenger

"What!" Patrick said. It was almost a shout. He frowned.

Beth wanted to explain that it wasn't magic or spirits. It was a mechanical toy. But before she could speak, a trumpet sounded.

It startled them.

A Mongol warrior burst through the doors of the throne room.

Beth and Patrick recognized him. He was the man who had grabbed Beth. He had also said Patrick was evil. It was Koke.

The warrior stumbled. Something was strange about his clothes.

Beth gasped.

Koke's tunic was soaked in blood. An arrow had been shot through the man's shoulder.

"He's hurt," Beth said. She turned to the Polos. "Someone help him!"

Beth started forward, but Amaffeo put a hand on her shoulder. "Wait," he said. "To help him would make him look weak. Let him speak."

The man limped toward the throne. One hand clutched the arrow at his shoulder.

He fell on the first stair of the platform. He bowed at the feet of Kublai Khan.

"What is it, Koke?" the khan asked. "Tell me."

"Three thousand Arab soldiers march toward Shangdu," the wounded man said. "Four hundred Mongol rebels lead them on horses."

The khan rose to his feet. He said, "They do the bidding of my enemy—Baraq!"

Koke said, "Even now they ram the gate."

A smile crept over Kublai Khan's face. His whole body seemed to glow. It was as if the threat of war brought him to life.

He sat down again and rubbed his chin. He waved his hand at the three men with the pointy beards. They rushed forward.

He said to them, "We must talk."

Beth looked at poor Koke still on the floor.

Then the khan seemed to remember him and said, "You may go, Koke."

Not even a "thank you," Beth thought.

The khan and the three Chinese men spoke in low voices. Koke struggled to his feet.

Koke took a few steps. He looked at Beth. Then his eyes rolled upward. He fell to the floor.

Beth couldn't stand seeing him hurt.

"He needs help," she said. "Somebody do something!"

Patrick came over to her. He asked, "Do the Chinese have doctors?" he asked.

The Polos came close too.

"Where are our medicines?" Marco asked his father and uncle.

Amaffeo said, "I will send a servant to get our belongings."

Beth put her hand on Koke's forehead. "He's burning with fever!" she said.

The warrior slowly opened his eyes. He

looked into her face.

"We'll help you," she said.

Koke's eyes moved to Patrick's face. Suddenly the warrior looked fearful. He rose up with the little strength he had.

"The devil boy!" Koke shouted. "The boy who came from nowhere! He brings this evil."

The warrior pointed at Patrick. The man shook all over. Then he fell back in a faint.

Beth looked at Patrick, who looked worried. She looked at Marco Polo, who frowned. Then they looked over at Kublai Khan. His eyes were on them.

"Guards," the khan called. "Take these Christian shamans away. Make sure they can't escape!"

Good-bye

"Is there anything else in that bag?" Beth asked Patrick.

She hoped Mr. Whittaker had given them an extra gift. She wanted to give one to the guard outside the door. Maybe then he would tell them what was going on.

"Let me look," Patrick said.

While he did that, Beth looked around the room again. She and Patrick were alone in a small room. The walls were brick, held up by thick beams of wood. One small window was set high in the wall. The door was shut. There was no escape.

Patrick looked inside the bag. "Aha! Here's one last gift," he said and pulled out a small package. It was wrapped in bright yellow paper.

"What does the tag say?" Beth asked.

"I don't know. It's written in a foreign language," he said. "It looks like Chinese picture words."

Patrick squeezed the package.

"It feels like another book," he said. "Should we open it?"

"Not yet," said Beth. "Maybe we should show it to the guard—it might be a message to him."

There were voices outside of the door.

"Shh," Patrick whispered.

Beth moved to the door. She pressed her ear against it. Then she jumped back as it swung open.

Niccolò Polo stepped through the door. "I have spoken to Kublai Khan."

Beth said, "Will he let us out of here?"

Niccolò frowned. "No," he said, "but he has allowed me to come and say good-bye."

"Good-bye!" Patrick said. "You're leaving us here?"

"We have no choice," Niccolò said. "Kublai Khan has ordered me, Marco, and Amaffeo to serve as his messengers. We are going to warn the other cities about Baraq."

"What about us?" Beth asked. "Why can't we go with you?"

"The khan is worried about your powers,"

Marco said. "He's afraid to let you leave. You may use your powers against him."

"But we don't have that kind of power," Beth said.

Niccolò shook his head. "Maybe not. But he thinks you do. And so you will be his guests here."

The cousins groaned.

Niccolò placed one hand on each of their shoulders. "Don't worry," he said. "You will go to school with Kublai Khan's own grandchildren."

Patrick's expression turned from sadness to panic. "We'll have to stay in China?" he asked. "And go to *school*?"

Beth said, "We can't stay here! We must help Albert!"

Niccolò looked at the cousins with

curiosity. Then he smiled.

"You're strange children," Niccolò said.

"May we say good-bye to Marco and Amaffeo?" Beth asked.

"Kublai Khan will allow you to see them before they leave," Niccolò said. "But the guard must go with you. He will take you at the right time."

Early the next morning, the cousins and the Polos said their good-byes.

"I'll remember you whenever I write in my diary," Marco said.

"I'll remember you every time I play the game in the pool," Patrick said.

Marco gave Patrick a curious glance. Then he got on his horse.

Amaffeo and Niccolò rode out the gate first. Marco turned to wave one last time. Then he left Shangdu.

The guard led Patrick and Beth back to their room. The cousins stepped inside. They watched the door as it swung shut. They heard the guard quickly bolt the door.

They were trapped, again.

"You're taller than I thought," said a soft voice. It came from behind them.

The cousins spun around.

Sitting on a bed was a Mongol girl.

The Princess

The girl stood up and bowed. Her little hat almost fell off.

"It is an honor to meet you," she said. "I am called Beki." The girl bowed again.

"Hi," said Patrick. "I'm Patrick." He gave her a half bow.

"I'm Beth," said Beth. She studied the girl. Beki looked to be about her age.

"Weren't you in the throne room yesterday?" Beth asked.

"Yes," Beki said. "I saw all that happened. And I want to thank you."

"Thank *us*?" Patrick said. "For which part? Looking foolish with our nails or getting locked up?"

"You were brave," Beki said. "You told my grandfather about Jesus."

"Your grandfather is Kublai Khan?" Beth asked.

"Yes," Beki said. "And he can be very stubborn. He won't listen to the truth about Jesus. But he listens to the yellow lamas. And you proved them wrong."

"We scared everyone with a toy chicken," Patrick said. "And it was just a simple windup toy."

Beki's eyes widened. "That is a *toy* in your land?" she asked.

"Sure," Patrick said.

Beki's eyes sparkled. "I would love to see more of your toys," she said. "They must be amazing!"

Patrick smiled and said, "I wish I had a laptop to show you. Or even a cell phone."

"Lap top? Sell fone?" she said. The words didn't mean anything to Beki. But she looked impressed.

"Never mind," Beth said. "Why did you come to see us?"

"I have something to show you," Beki said.

She reached for a bag that was next to her on the bed. She pulled out a golden tablet. "You must take this," Beki said.

Patrick and Beth gasped.

"Is that a golden tablet of Kublai Khan?" Patrick asked.

"Better," Beki said. "It is the golden tablet of *Genghis* Khan and Kublai Khan. Genghis was the first and most powerful Mongol khan. He was my great-great-grandfather. He gave this to Kublai Khan's mother. I am named after her. She gave it to my grandfather, who gave it to me. Now I am giving it to you."

She gave the tablet to Beth.

The gold felt smooth and cool to Beth's touch. "Why are you giving it to us?" Beth asked.

"Because you'll need it when Baraq's warriors come," Beki said. "They will try to kill grandfather. If they do, you will not be safe without a tablet from Genghis. He is still feared, even though he is dead."

"But what about you?" Beth said. "You

won't be safe either."

"No one will harm me," Beki said. "I am the great-great-granddaughter of Genghis Khan. The Mongol leaders treat royal girls well. They hope I will marry one of their sons."

Beth gave the golden tablet to Patrick. He looked it over. Then he put it inside his wool bag. His face lit up.

"Wait," he said. He took out the present that was wrapped in yellow paper. The tag written in Chinese hung from the top.

"Can you read this?" he asked Beki. "It might be for you."

Beki took the gift. She felt the yellow paper and then she inspected the tag.

"Thank you," Beki said. "This is Chinese. My grandfather is making me learn it."

Beki read the tag out loud, "To Beki, a daughter of the true Khan, Jesus Christ."

"So it *is* for you!" Beth said.

"Mr. Whittaker knew we would meet," Patrick added.

Beki look confused. "Mr. Wit-tock-air?"

"He's a friend of ours," Patrick said.

"Open the package," said Beth.

Beki gently peeled off the paper. She held the book and pressed it to her. Her eyes filled with tears.

"A Bible!" she said. Beki flipped the book open. "It's written in Chinese. Now I can learn more about being a Christian."

Beth glanced at the Bible. The Chinese characters were stacked top to bottom. She also saw a card fall out of the Bible. She picked it up. A note was written on it in English.

"It's from Mr. Whittaker," Beth said. "It says, 'Hurry up, you two. You have a golden tablet. Use the nails to make a ladder. Get out of the palace. NOW!'"

The Nest

"Why didn't I think of that?" Patrick asked. "We could have escaped last night."

"Good thing we didn't," Beth said. "Or we wouldn't have met Beki."

Patrick picked up the hammer. He pounded the first long nail partway into the wood beam. Then he stood on that nail. Quickly he hammered all ten nails in partway. He nailed them into both sides of the beam. The nails were now footholds and handholds. They weren't very strong, but they would do.

Finally Patrick reached the window at the top of the wall. He looked down at the two girls.

"Beki," he said, "how does the window open? It's the only way out."

"You can push them out," she said.

Patrick looked closely at the wood around the window. The wood was only notched. He pushed on the frame. The window came out easily.

If they had used nails, Patrick thought, himself, *it would have been harder to escape.*

He called to Beth, "Come on up, Beth. We can get to the roof through this opening."

Beth and Beki hugged good-bye.

"Thanks for the golden tablet," Beth said

to the Mongol princess. "It may save our lives—and another man's life as well."

Beki nodded and smiled. "Thank you for the Bible," she said. "It will save my life."

The cousins reached the palace roof. They could see for miles.

"Baraq's army is coming from the east," Patrick said. "They'll reach the gate in no time. . . . By the way, are you *sure* Mongols didn't have airplanes?"

"Don't be silly!" Beth said. "The Wright brothers flew the first plane in the twentieth century, not the thirteenth. Plus it was in North Carolina—not North China."

"Silly, huh?" Patrick said. "Then what are those two black things in the sky?"

Beth looked east. She had to cover her eyes from the sun's rays. She gasped.

"They're eagles."

"Really *big* eagles," Patrick said.

"It can't be! Those are *rocs*," Beth said. "But rocs aren't real. They're made up in books and fairy tales! They *can't* exist."

"These do," Patrick said. "And they're coming right at us!"

The rocs swooped down near Patrick and Beth. The giant birds flapped their wings for a moment. They hung in the sky and eyed the cousins.

Patrick was worried. "Do we look like giant worms?" he asked.

The wind from the flapping wings blew Beth's hair. She stared at one of their huge heads. She guessed the roc's beak could tear apart a car. She stepped backward, trying to get away. But there was nowhere to go but down.

"What do we do?" Beth asked. "Should we roll off the roof?"

"It's too high—" Patrick said.

Suddenly a roc swooped and scooped Patrick up by the arms. Its claws wrapped around him. They were surprisingly warm.

He heard Beth scream and saw that she had been snatched up too.

Patrick wriggled with all his might.

"Let me go, you birdbrain!" he shouted.

Then Patrick realized he was already a hundred yards above the palace. To fall would mean broken bones, if not death.

"Don't let me go!" he shouted.

His stomach lurched. He closed his eyes. *God, please help us,* he prayed.

When he looked down again, the rebel army

was below him.

The birds flew fast and far. Over the plains. Over the Great Wall.

Patrick felt as if he were in a wind tunnel. When he breathed, great gushes of air filled his lungs.

The wind burned his eyes, and so he closed them again.

The bird's talons squeezed him tightly under his arms. He was afraid his arms would fall asleep.

Finally the bird began to fly lower. Patrick opened his eyes and looked ahead. They had come to the red cliffs.

Is it taking us to the Imagination Station? he wondered. *Did Mr. Whittaker arrange for*

the rocs to do that?

Then he saw a giant bird nest on a cliff
ledge. It wasn't made from small sticks
and thin twigs; it was made from giant tree
trunks and thick branches. It was lined with
sheepskin.

Two baby rocs sat in the nest. Their
feathers were fluffy and white. Their eyes and
beaks were black. They stretched out their
thin necks. They opened wide their beaks.

"Aaw! Aaw!" the baby birds cried.

Uh-oh, thought Patrick. *We're going to be
bird food.*

Beth saw the cuddly eaglets. They reminded
her of Easter chicks.

She saw the first roc drop Patrick into the
nest. Then the parent roc flew away.

How cute, Beth thought. *The rocs must think we're their babies. They want Patrick and me to live in their nest. They want to take care of us.*

She saw Patrick land feetfirst. He rubbed one shoulder and then the next. She was glad to see that he still had the wool bag.

The second roc dropped Beth and swooped away. She landed on her side. The sheepskin softened the blow. Then she felt something poke her through the cushion. A branch had scraped her leg. She started to bleed.

"Ouch!" she said.

The little rocs wobbled toward Beth.

They didn't look as cuddly up close. They were bigger than full-grown geese. Their eyes were fierce like a weasel's. Their beaks were hooked and sharp.

One of the beaks grabbed Beth. She moved to one side. The bird caught the edge of her dress.

"It's got me!" she shouted to Patrick. "Help!"

"Watch out!" Patrick yelled. He was carrying a large branch in his arms.

"Yaw!" he shouted.

The baby roc let go of Beth's dress. It jumped back at the sudden shout. Patrick swung the branch. It just missed the eaglet's beak.

The little roc squealed.

EEEP!

It sounded scared.

"Thanks," Beth said to Patrick. He helped her to her feet. The cut on her leg hurt.

"Let's get out of here," Patrick said. "They want to make us a meal."

Just then a shadow covered the nest. The cousins looked up.

"Yikes," Patrick said. "One of the parents is back."

The long, curved talons of the roc lowered toward them.

Patrick and Beth froze in fear. They dropped down and covered their faces with their arms.

They waited for claws to dig into their skin.

"No . . . you . . . don't!" came a man's shout.

The cousins looked up.

Suddenly a silver sword slashed the air above them. The sword hit the bird's claws, and the bird cried out.

Raaaw!

Beth looked over at a man wearing full chain mail and leggings. Then she saw his face. He looked very familiar.

"Who is that?" Patrick asked. "It looks like a young Mr. Whittaker!"

"It's the knight!" Beth said.

"But where is his armor?" asked Patrick. "He's going to need it!"

Raaaw! Raaaw!

The roc called as it swooped down again. This time it came headfirst.

It opened its yellow beak wide.

Beth saw the bird's throat. The opening was large enough to swallow a man in one bite.

"Look out!" she cried.

The knight turned just in time. He swung the sword with both hands.

Bam!

The sword hit the roc's beak—and bounced off. The roc backed off, but it still hovered over the nest.

"To the edge of the nest!" the knight shouted. He pointed to a spot near the cliff wall. "There!"

The cousins scrambled to their feet. They raced to the edge of the nest. The bottom of the cliff was far away.

"Does he want us to jump?" Patrick asked.

"That'll kill us," Beth said.

"The machine!" the man shouted and pointed.

Another shadow passed overhead. Parent roc number two was back.

Raaaw! Raaaw!

In an instant, the nest was a whirlwind of action. Flapping wings. Slashing sword. Snapping beaks.

Patrick and Beth panicked. They didn't dare

jump. What did the knight want them to do?

Then the Imagination Station appeared at the edge of the nest. It seemed to hang halfway on the nest and halfway in the air. The door was open for them.

Beth didn't move. Was the Imagination Station a flying machine? Would it fall if she got in?

"What are you waiting for?" Patrick shouted.

She had to believe it was safe. She leaped in through the door.

Patrick was about to jump, but he turned to the knight. He was still fighting the rocs.

"Are you coming?" Patrick asked.

"Go! Save Albert!" the knight called to him. "And may God be with you!"

Patrick flung himself at the Imagination Station's door.

● ● ●

Patrick joined Beth inside the Imagination Station. He settled into a black seat. The door closed. The red button on the dashboard blinked.

The cousins sighed with relief.

"Good," Beth said, "you still have the bag."

Patrick looked down. He had forgotten he was holding it.

He looked toward the closed door. "What about the knight? We should help him," Patrick said.

"We can't," she said. "He told us to help Albert."

Beth pushed the red button.

Everything went black.

In the Dark

Patrick blinked. The darkness wouldn't go away.

He stood on stony ground. The Imagination Station was gone.

"Patrick?" Beth whispered next to him.

"Where are we?" she asked. "This isn't the workshop at Whit's End."

"I know," Patrick said.

Patrick heard the echo of his voice. The air around him was damp and cool. He narrowed his eyes.

The darkness turned to deep blacks. Then grays. Then the blacks and grays took shape.

Patrick reached out and took a step. His fingers touched a rock wall. It was bumpy and slimy.

"We're in a cave," Patrick said.

"A cave!" Beth said. "What cave? Where is it?"

"You mean '*When is it*?'" Patrick said. "I think we jumped to another time."

For the next part of the adventure, go to TheImaginationStation.com. Click on the cover of *Revenge of the Red Knight*.

Secret Word Puzzle

Fill in the crossword puzzle on the next page. The letters in the shaded boxes will spell out a secret word.

Write those letters in the boxes below the puzzle grid. The answer is the secret word and the name of a valuable book.

Down

1. The first name of the khan who Marco Polo met. (page 55)
2. The first name of Marco's father. (page 41)
3. The name of the man who needs Mr. Whittaker's help. (page 3)

Across

1. The name of the country that has "the Great Wall." (page 24)

2 The name of the Mongol princess. (page 93)

3 The name of the Mongol warrior who was shot with an arrow. (page 82)

4 The first name of Marco's uncle. (page 41)

1 down	1 across	2 across	2 down	4 across

FOCUS ON THE FAMILY®

No matter who you are, what you're going through, or what challenges your family may be facing, we're here to help. With practical resources —like our toll-free Family Help Line, counseling, and Web sites— we're committed to providing trustworthy, biblical guidance, and support.

Focus on the Family Clubhouse Jr.

Creative stories, fascinating articles, puzzles, craft ideas, and more are packed into each issue of *Focus on the Family Clubhouse Jr.*® magazine. You'll love the way this bright and colorful magazine reinforces biblical values and helps boys and girls (ages 3–7) explore their world. **Subscribe now at Clubhousejr.com.**

Focus on the Family Clubhouse

Through an appealing combination of encouraging content and entertaining activities, *Focus on the Family Clubhouse*® magazine (ages 8–12) will help your children—or kids you care about—develop a strong Christian foundation. **Subscribe now at Clubhousemagazine.com.**

AUTHOR MARIANNE HERING
is former editor of *Focus on the Family Clubhouse* ® magazine. She has written more than a dozen children's books. She likes to take walks in the rain with her golden retriever, Chase.

ILLUSTRATOR DAVID HOHN
draws and paints books, posters, and projects of all kinds. He works from his studio in Portland, Oregon.

AUTHOR PAUL McCUSKER
is a writer and director for *Adventures in Odyssey* ®. He has written over fifty novels and dramas. Paul likes peanut butter-and-banana sandwiches and wears his belt backward.